Herbster Readers

HAPPY NEW YEAR, HERBIE BEAR!

Written by Joanne Meier and Cecilia Minden • Illustrated by Bob Ostrom
Created by Herbie J. Thorpe

ABOUT THE AUTHORS

Joanne Meier, PhD, has worked as an elementary school teacher, university professor, and researcher. She earned her BA in early childhood education from the University of South Carolina, and her MEd and PhD in education from the University of Virginia. She currently works as a literacy consultant for schools and private organizations. Joanne lives in Virginia with her husband Eric, daughters Kella and Erin, two cats, and a gerbil.

Cecilia Minden, PhD, is the former director of the Language and Literacy Program at the Harvard Graduate School of Education. She is now a reading consultant for school and library publications. She earned her PhD in reading education from the University of Virginia. Cecilia and her husband, Dave Cupp, live outside Chapel Hill, North Carolina. They enjoy sharing their love of reading with their grandchildren, Chelsea and Qadir.

ABOUT THE ILLUSTRATOR

Bob Ostrom has been illustrating children's books for nearly twenty years. A graduate of the New England School of Art & Design at Suffolk University, Bob has worked for such companies as Disney, Nickelodeon, and Cartoon Network. He lives in North Carolina with his wife Melissa and three children, Will, Charlie, and Mae.

ABOUT THE SERIES CREATOR

Herbie J. Thorpe had long envisioned a beginning-readers' series about a fun, energetic bear with a big imagination. Herbie is a book lover and an avid supporter of libraries and the role they play in fostering the love of reading. He consults with librarians and matches them with the perfect books for their students and patrons. He lives in Louisiana with his wife Misty and their daughter Carson.

The Child's World®

Published in the United States of America by The Child's World®
1980 Lookout Drive • Mankato, MN 56003-1705
800-599-READ • www.childsworld.com

Acknowledgments
The Child's World®: Mary Berendes, Publishing Director
The Design Lab: Kathleen Petelinsek, Design;
Kari Tobin, Page Production
Artistic Assistant: Richard Carbajal

Library of Congress Cataloging-in-Publication Data
Meier, Joanne D.
  Happy new year, Herbie Bear! / by Joanne Meier and Cecilia
Minden ; illustrated by Bob Ostrom.
    p. cm. — (Herbster readers)
  ISBN 978-1-60253-220-5 (library bound : alk. paper)
  [1. New Year—Fiction. 2. Bears—Fiction.] I. Minden, Cecilia.
II. Ostrom, Bob, ill. III. Title. IV. Series.

  PZ7.M5148Hap 2009
  [E]—dc22   2009003981

"Tonight's the night!" said Herbie Bear.

Herbie was going to stay up late.

Really, really late.

It was December 31. It was New Year's Eve.

8

Herbie's dad said Herbie could stay up.

They would celebrate the New Year together.

"The New Year begins at midnight," said Dad. "That's pretty late!"

Dad looked at the clock. "It might be hard to stay awake that long," he said.

"I'll stay awake!" said Herbie.

"I'm going to drop a ball!"

Dad laughed. "We don't drop a ball, Herbie."

17

"We'll watch a ball drop," said Dad.

"Huh?" said Herbie. "That sounds boring."

"It's a special ball," explained Dad.

"It's in New York City."

"Well," said Herbie. "At least I get to stay up late! That part should be fun."

Herbie and Dad had a good time.

They played games.

They had hot chocolate.

They watched a funny movie.

Herbie fell asleep. It was 11:30 P.M.

"Happy New Year," whispered Dad.

He carried Herbie to bed.

Herbie just smiled.